The Timely Arrival of Barnabas Bead

THE TIMELY ARRIVAL OF
BARNABAS
BEAD

A. S. PETERSON

TALES OF AN UNREMEMBERED COUNTRY

Cover design © 2014 by Chris Stewart
Illustrations © 2015 by Joe Sutphin

Published by
Rabbit Room Press
3321 Stephens Hill Lane
Cane Ridge, TN 37013
info@rabbitroom.com

ISBN: 978-0-9863818-2-9

Printed in the United States of America

There are more things in heaven and earth, Horatio,
than are dreamt of in your philosophy.

William Shakespeare

IN THE LONG AND STORIED LIFE OF COLONEL Barnabas Bead, there was no winter either so hateful or so magical as that which blew through the Cumberland Gap in the last days of 1864. It was aloof and amoral, as winters have always been, for while spring, summer, and autumn have their virtues and give their particular gifts of life, warmth, and beauty, winter abides no sentiment; she enters a room stiffly and coolly, quieting everyone to whispers, staring down her slim white nose as the world quivers before her. The season of Colonel Bead's salvation was a tyrant more uncaring even than all her sisters before. She hewed upon a direct line between political towers, taking no side at all, neither Union nor Confederate. In her march toward spring she laid men of all colors and creeds in their graves, and to look on her passage and see the sorrowful days of her procession, you'd not have thought anything good could come of her. But as December stretched its arms and yawned, there followed in the train of winter's gown a flicker of old magic that Barnabas Bead would not forget.

As Colonel Bead huddled by the dying embers of a fire in the shadow of Cumberland Mountain, he wondered not for the first time (nor the last) how he had ever strayed so far from the sea. His father, Howell Alan Bead (called Howlin' Bead by those who knew him) had been a sailing man and had spent his days before the mast waging the War of Independence. After the war, Howlin' had aimed to settle into a life of gentle labors and quiet days, but only a step from taking that well-trodden road, he had been diverted by the promise of a fair ship departing Savannah in search of parts wild and unmapped. The ship was a French privateersman by the name of *Esprit de la Mer*, and Howlin' Bead never spoke of his years aboard her without something very like a song in his voice, for he claimed that the ship had sailed upon the seas of other worlds entire, and plumbed the depths of lost oceans, and visited exotic lands that only the tales of Araby or ancient Homer rightly describe. In time, the *Esprit de la Mer* returned him to the shores of the known world and, having seen many mysteries to which no road leads, he put his foot at last upon the well-trodden path and married a widow and founded a family which produced a long string of Beads that ended with the birth of Barnabas Alan.

In Barnabas' youth, his father had regaled him each night with tales of the high seas and all the fine adventures that lay behind him, and in his sleeping the young boy sailed a dreamland of his father's making. The sea called to Barnabas when he was a lad of fourteen, and when he left home to chase it, he told neither his father nor his mother nor any one of his seven brothers or sisters where he was going. He bundled his clothes and a flint knife and three strips of dried beef into a sack and walked out onto the front porch of the Georgia farmhouse.

"Paw," he said.

"Why you got that sack?" said Howlin' Bead.

Barnabas shrugged. "Tell Maw I'll be back for supper." Thereupon, Barnabas Bead walked off the well-trodden path onto which his father had borne him. He took to the sea like Howlin' had, and while he worked as an able seaman on merchantmen between worlds Old and New, he kept one eye keen to every ship he met, wondering always if it would bear the name that carried the song of his father's tales: *Esprit de la Mer.* But the work of young seamen soon makes old salt of them; it wears dreams away as it does innocence and inhibition, and after years enough before the mast, then amidships, and then finally in staterooms of his own, Barnabas Bead grew lonesome for the well-trodden path and sailed for home.

When he returned from his long sojourn he stepped up onto the front porch of the Georgia farmhouse he had departed years before and dropped his sack. He saw his mother's form silhouetted in the window and called out, "I'm home, Maw. Is supper ready?"

His answer came in the form of a musket-ball through the front window. Crack said the old muzzleloader, and crack said the window, and then "Damn!" said Barnabas Bead and down he went with three ounces and a half of lead ball in his shoulder. It is a terrible thing to be shot at all, and it is an even more terrible thing to be shot by an old woman whom you believe to be your mother—but is not.

The old woman waddled through the farmhouse door with a giant musket settled into the pocket of her shoulder. "You dead?" she croaked.

"I come to see my Maw and Paw."

The woman set the butt of the musket down on the porch floor. She reached into her apron and withdrew a powder horn and uncorked it and tapped a thimbleful of black powder into the muzzle of the gun.

"What are you doing?" cried Barnabas Bead. He lay sprawled on his back and held his right hand up to cover the thumb-sized hole in his left shoulder.

"I shoot any man comes on my porch without leave. Them as don't die, I shoot twice." She gnawed a patch of wadding off her apron and began to pack the barrel.

Disinclined to lie in wait of aid, Barnabas Bead leapt to his feet and ran.

What became of Maw and Paw Bead he could not discover, and he mourned the loss of his family so badly that he signed up for a new one: that of the Army of Tennessee. The army took him in without hesitation, sewed up his shoulder, and made him a colonel.

Soon afterward, the War Between the States caught up with Colonel Bead and dragged him wherever it went. On many a Sunday afternoon he led the boys and men of the Confederacy down well-trodden roads toward small towns and barren ridges that he was told (by General Felix Zollicoffer) would prove to be the very keys of victory against the North. But on those ridges and in those towns the war shook his boys and rent them, and though Colonel Barnabas Bead watched sharply for the gates of victory to open, he never saw the door crack an inch—though he did see many of his finest boys cracked open nevermore to be shut.

By 1863 he had grown tired of chasing the keys of victory and he thought to get himself clear of the search by resigning his commission. He spent three days composing an elaborate letter of his intent and three days more working up the courage required to deliver it—during which time he often fell into heated arguments with himself.

"Barnabas you've written the damned thing, and now you've got to march in there and give it to him!"

"I can't!" Barnabas wailed at himself.

"You can!" Barnabas yelled back.

"He'll call me a coward!"

"I don't care what he calls us. We're tired and too old for this business."

"He won't care."

"Show him your teeth. They don't want colonels with bad teeth."

"That's true."

At that moment, Lieutenant Horton Adams, Bead's adjutant, happened to pass his colonel's tent. He overheard this argument and was determined to rise to the defense of the commanding officer he had served loyally for nearly two years. He flung open the flap of the tent and strode in with one hand placed threateningly on the hilt of his saber. When he discovered that the tent was empty—save only the old man he'd entered to defend—Adams stopped short and held himself very still. In confusion, he cast about suspiciously with his eyes.

"What is it, Adams," said Colonel Bead.

"I, uh—is everything all right, suh?"

"Of course it isn't. Why do you ask?

"Forgive me, suh. I perceived that there was— ah, I thought I heard—"

"Look at my teeth, Adams." Bead leaned over (for he was considerably tall) and stretched his mouth wide open. Without hesitation Adams leaned in and inspected each tooth with the meticulous eye of an officer. When he had completed his inspection, he snapped his heels and grunted. "Well?" said Colonel Bead.

"Suh, yoo-uh teeth ah impeccable."

Knowing his teeth to be mostly missing or mostly rotten, Colonel Bead had not expected this answer. "Are you sure, Adams?"

"Yes, suh. They ah the teeth of a lion."

Colonel Bead picked up a hand mirror from his desk and inspected his teeth himself. "Adams, did you know that my father had a tooth made from the ankle-bone of a star?"

"Suh?"

"He was a sailor, Adams, and I was too, you know—but he sailed farther than any man I ever heard of. Beyond Good Hope, beyond the Galapagos, beyond India and Japan, even across the Sea of Tranquility—though he was never precise on where that was. He told me that he once came to blows with a man who wore a veil of fire and held a shard of lightning in his hand."

"Lightning, suh?"

"In his hand. Like sword. Can you imagine that, Adams?"

"No, suh."

"They tussled, and when my father had nearly bested him—using nothing more than an old bucket and a yard of iron chain—a star fell from the sky and knocked out one of my father's teeth."

Adams sighed and his shoulders sagged and his eyes inspected the tent above and around Colonel Bead's head. "You don't say, suh?"

"I do say, and so did my father, whom I never knew to lie. When the man with the veil of fire saw that the tooth was lost, he scolded the star and broke off a piece of its ankle, which he fashioned into a tooth and gave to my father."

"An incredible tale, suh."

"Here's a picture." Colonel Bead reached into his coat pocket and withdrew a battered old daguerreotype, which he promptly handed to Adams. It was a likeness of a middle-aged man wearing an surly smile, and set in the middle of the smile was a brightly polished metal tooth that shone like—well, even Adams

had to admit that it had a star-like quality. Adams snapped his heels and grunted.

"Will that be all, suh?"

"Yes, very well, Adams. I have a letter to deliver. Will you excuse me? Dismissed." Bead looked softly at the daguerreotype and ran his finger across its silvery surface. *Esprit de la Mer.* He could almost hear the music of his father's tale. As he tilted the daguerreotype from side to side, the tooth twinkled at him. Then he slipped the picture into his pocket, took up his letter of resignation, and went in search of General Zollicoffer. The path between the tents of the Confederate camp was worn down to muddy ruts. Bead cursed the path and walked wide of it to keep his boots clean.

"Bead!" shouted General Felix Zollicoffer when Colonel Bead entered the command tent. "Bead, what are you doing here? Who's defending the ridge at Heathcliff's Bluff? Do you realize that Heathcliff's Bluff could be the key to victory against the North? Have you set picket lines? If the Union makes a show, it'll be hellfire and widows' weeping from here to the Virginia line! Zebulon tells me they've got three companies of artillery hid in these hills and his men have seen the ghosts of Hooker's cavalry galloping in the trees. Why, you must be a ghost yourself, Bead! That's it exactly, for I can think of no other reason why you should be here to haunt me other than that you are dead in the defense of Heathcliff's Bluff!"

"Sorry, sir."

"So you are dead then?" Had Felix Zollicoffer been a Catholic, he would have made the sign of the cross, but he was only a Congregationalist and didn't believe in the sign of the cross (or ghosts) so he took a drink of brandy instead.

"Well no, sir. I'm afraid not."

"Damn."

"Sir?"

"This had better be important, Bead."

"I'd like to resign my commission, sir."

General Felix Zollicoffer took another drink of brandy and then made the sign of the cross. "What did you say, Bead?"

"My commission, sir. I think I'd like to give it back. I've got an old shoulder wound, sir. I think I'd like to go back to the sea for a while. And I've got bad teeth, you know. Even Adams says so." Colonel Bead leaned over the desk and opened his mostly-toothless maw for General Zollicoffer to inspect.

In the twenty minutes that followed, Colonel Bead was called a coward, an ingrate, a damned coward, a blue-blooded sympathizer, a dirty abolitionist, a godless bastard, a Frenchman, a Tory, a Spaniard, a spaniel, a confounded boob, a congressman, a man of low moral character, a heathen, a papist, a Lutheran, and a good many other things that General Felix Zollicoffer could not pronounce correctly in his brandy-fueled rage. And though Colonel Bead was not permitted to resign his commission, he was immediately relieved of the keys of victory. General Zollicoffer reassigned him to a post from which he hoped that Bead would never return and for which he hoped that no useful commanding officer would ever be required. Within an hour of being shorn of his command, Colonel Bead, along with Lieutenant Adams (who stubbornly refused to be relieved of his own post), was marching east toward the Gap of the Cumberland.

"This is a good move for us, Adams."

"Yes, suh."

"A quiet spot in the mountains."

"Yes, suh."

"And when the war is sorted out, Adams, I shall take you to see the ocean."

"The ocean, suh?"

"Yes, Adams. The Atlantic."

"All things accounted, suh, when the wo-uh concludes, I intend to set fuh South Carolina."

"Of course, you will. I apologize, Adams. But if you ever go so far as Charleston, do go to the sea."

"Yes, suh."

"Did I ever tell you that my father was a seaman?"

Adams shoulders sagged and he sighed and he shook his head slowly from side to side. "No, suh."

"He sailed on a ship called the *Esprit de la Mer*. Isn't that a lovely name?" (Yes, suh.) "And he told me that the captain was a fiddle player. He'd wake in the night at times and hear her playing, the notes humming in muffled tones through the bulkheads."

"Did you say 'huh,' suh?"—by which he meant "her, sir."

"I did, Adams. Indeed I did. He told me she had red hair and almost never spoke—though at night her fiddle spoke for her. He said the music of the fiddle drove the sails on windless seas and blew the *Esprit* to lands never seen by living men. What do you supposed he meant by that, Adams."

"I don't know, suh."

"Neither do I. But I listen for the music all the same. I spent fifteen years at sea, Adams. I worked on seven fine ships, and had twelve able captains, and every night of those years I fell asleep listening for the music."

"Did you he-uh it, suh? The music."

Colonel Bead frowned and looked down at his feet. "Are we still on the path, Adams. I lose sight of it sometimes."

"I believe so, suh."

Colonel Bead sighed and looked around him as if he had forgotten where he ought to be. Ahead of them the road weaved on through the hills, rising up toward higher crests in the distance. To the south, the land dropped away into a valley and the glimmer of water winked up out of the deepest reaches of it.

"This way, Adams. I suppose it's up this way."

THEY WERE FOUR DAYS ON THE ROAD WHEN THEY came to three shabby buildings that together accorded themselves the town of Harrowgate. The first building was a general store that was boarded up, disused, and guarded by a feral mule. Adams offered to shoot the creature but Colonel Bead forbade him unless the mule should attack unprovoked.

The second building was a wheelwright's carpentry that lay besieged by scores of lopsided, unfinished, and ill-engineered wagon wheels. The structure of the building itself seemed so inextricably supported by spokes, runners, and spare parts that Colonel Bead warned Adams not to touch any of them, fearing that the disturbance of a single wooden stave would result in an avalanche and put an end to one third of the town's infrastructure. The third building was an outhouse; Colonel Bead and Lieutenant Adams found it in working order.

The town of Harrowgate lay only a few miles south of the great Gap of the Cumberland and Colonel Bead hoped to make a successful liaison with the locals before continuing to his new post in the mountains.

"Is anyone there?" the colonel called out. He looked with great disappointment upon the derelict general store and its loyal guard, for he had hoped the close proximity of general goods would ease the difficulty of such a remote post. It seemed entirely likely to him that there lay within the building an abandoned sack of coffee beans waiting only to be reclaimed from ruin and put to good use each morning at breakfast. As he considered whether or not to brave the ferocity of the mule in order to mount an expedition of the place, a voice rose up in answer to his call.

"Which way you goin' to?"

Adams' eyes peeled back wide and white and he stared at the mule as if Balaam's own ass had come forth to prophesy against them. He raised his pistol and said. "Shall I an-suh the beast, suh?"

Colonel Bead took a step toward the animal and called out, "To the Gap." He spoke loudly, as though the mule might be deaf as well as vocal.

The mule bared its teeth and shook it's head and bellowed a fearsome bray.

"I'd get no closer I was you." A stranger stepped from around the corner of the wheelwright's carpentry and shook his head at the mule. "He eat Cornelius three weeks ago. He likely take a bite out of you you let him. To the Gap, eh?"

Adams lowered his pistol but kept his other hand on his saber. Though it seemed clear it was the man who had spoken and not the mule, he kept one eye on the beast and it dwelt under his suspicion.

"I'm sorry about your friend," said Colonel Bead, removing his hat out of courtesy.

"Him? He ain't no friend."

"I was referring to Cornelius."

"Cornelius? Cornelius had it comin'. He'd crawl up on him and walk back and forth and pick and scrape at him and give him hell just for his own amusement. I knowed he'd get ate. Day it happened I heard him wailing. I come out to see was anything I could do, but he had him by the neck and shook him like a hound dog do a rattlesnake. When I come out again to go home he was swallered up clean and he been grinnin' about it ever since."

"Damn!" said Adams and took a sharp step away from the mule.

"Witness indeed that any man may come to an ignoble end," said Colonel Bead.

The wheelwright squinted and looked at Bead like he was an idiot, which he wasn't. "Cornelius was a calico tom."

Both Colonel Bead and Lieutenant Adams sighed, and Adams began to laugh nervously. Though neither of them approved of a cat-eating mule, it was a lesser evil than a man-eating mule-prophet, and so they chose to abide it without further interrogation.

The wheelwright slung a hatchet into the door-post where it quivered and sang out like a tuning fork. He spat a rope of black tobacco juice into the dirt and wiped his chin, then he looked up into the mountain pass above the town and chuckled to himself. "You fellas do better to turn back than go up in that Gap."

"Do soldiers at the garrison come to town often? I'd hoped to find a trading post here."

"I don't see no one."

"Perhaps that will change."

"Uh huh. Old Lady Winter goin' to take up in that Gap soon, colonel. When she do she'll most likely keep whatever and whoever she find up there."

Colonel Bead considered himself well acquainted with "Old Lady Winter" and was concerned instead with how to get to his post in the Gap as quickly as possible. He frowned and looked around at the town. They had arrived on the road from the west. Another road departed east, and another crossed between the outhouse and the general store running southwest to northeast. Each of the three paths before Colonel

Bead curled out of sight beneath the autumn trees and left him in doubt of which would take him up the mountain. The obvious choice was the northeast route, but many days spent marching blindly along country roads had taught him a valuable lesson: it is always best to ask. "The northeasterly road, here, where does that lead?"

"Where you want it to go?"

Colonel Bead smiled gently. "My aim is the Gap."

The wheelwright nodded his head and jerked his hatchet out of the doorpost. He cleaned the blade on his pant leg and sauntered into the middle of the road. "See there?" he said, raising the hatchet and swinging it in an arc that encompassed the countryside from southeast to southwest. Colonel Bead and Lieutenant Adams turned and looked. "Tennessee," said the wheelwright. "And look there." He pointed northeast and they looked there. "Virginia. And there." He pivoted on his heels and jabbed the hatchet northwest. "Kentucky."

"I see," said Colonel Bead.

The wheelwright chuckled and spat at the mule. "They's a crossroads, colonel. Places come from all

over to sit down up yonder and meet and rub shoulders. This road. That road. You see 'em, huh? Me too. But they's other roads run all around. They run so thin, they go between all things, like a spiderweb strung up across a deer run and don't show itself but in the evenin' sun. They's roads all over, colonel. Some like this one—" the wheelwright stamped his foot "—well trod. Some others not so well. You fellas go up into that Gap, you take care. Roads up there get thin. The White Lady makes 'em even thinner. You sometime take off one way and get somewhere you ain't figured to end up."

Colonel Bead stared up into the mountain gap and a sad, mournful shadow settled over his face. It was the look of a man for whom something precious had been lost but had also been forgotten and so was only mourned in brief moments when the wind brings him a familiar scent or the light reminds him of a barely remembered scene.

Adams looked from the wheelwright to the colonel in bewilderment. "Suh, if you could con-fuhm wheth-uh the road will go with-uh the colonel wills. We will be on ow-uh way."

"Take the northeast road, colonel. If you aim to keep to it, see you don't wander."

"Thank you," said Colonel Bead. "I fear I haven't asked your name, sir?"

The wheelwright grinned and spat. "Ask me again next time you come through Harrowgate." Then he retreated into his carpentry. The cat-eating mule bared its teeth and shuffled forward perilously. Colonel Bead and Lieutenant Adams took the northeast road into the Cumberland Gap.

LIEUTENANT ADAMS REFUSED TO PITCH CAMP UNTIL an hour nigh midnight, and once they did stop, Adams looked down the road behind them at regular intervals to be sure the mule had not followed. They had climbed high enough into the pass that the warm air of early autumn had deserted them for more southerly climes. The wind that remained nipped and chilled and Barnabas Bead felt in its touch the icy fingers of a dispassionate Lady teasing the hour of her advent. He kindled a fire to ward off her advances and leaned back on his pallet to sleep.

"We'll be there by noonday, I expect."

"I spect we will, suh."

"Do you suppose they'll be glad to see us, Adams?"

"I don't know, suh."

"I understand the garrison hasn't been reinforced in some time. The general told me the outfit is run by a young captain—his first command. I hope he doesn't take me as an insult to his dignity. You don't think he will, do you, Adams?"

"I spect not, suh.

"Do you see the north star, Adams?"

"Suh?"

"That one."

"Yes, suh."

"It never moves."

Adams narrowed his eyes and looked at the star suspiciously.

"At sea there aren't any roads to follow. Only stars. That's the thing about this Army business—I'm always looking down, looking to see I keep to the road. But at sea, you always have to look up. Isn't that something, Adams?"

"I suppose so, suh."

"Never mind your feet, Adams. Mind the stars. My father once told me he followed a star so closely that he sailed far enough to shake hands with Orion." Adams sighed and let his eyes slip closed. "I asked him how he got home again and he told me that it was no trouble at all, because from up there, the world too is a star, and one need only set a course by its faint light to sail back to it. Do you believe it, Adams? Adams?"

Adams was fast asleep. Colonel Bead pulled his blanket around him and stared into the night sky until he slept.

THE APPALACHIAN MOUNTAINS SPILL DOWN FROM New England in green billows. They wash over the continent in marbled swells of emerald and chartreuse, rising and falling, rippling through the bedrock with such patience and implacability that only an eye tuned to the waver of eternal rhythms can perceive the roll of their undulation or catch the thunder of their breaking and withdrawal. In another age, in the brief moment in which Cumberland Mountain rose up to the full height of its crest and reared its head and stretched its broad shoulders out across the firmament, it caught Orion's prowling eye. The hunter bent his bow and loosed. The missile hurled forth, exploding from the taut string like matter rejoicing in the moment of creation; it leaped through the unfathomed gaps between stars, ebullient, sizzle-hot, a feast of gases and fire, singing through the spaces between spaces, crackling and whistling in its song, racing across the arc of time, flashing through aeonian marvels and towering nebulae, fierce and bright as the dawn in its course until, in the blink of an eye, it smote the mountain. The monolithic left shoulder of the ridge,

pierced by the star-stroke, dropped heavily and the concussion of the blow rollicked over the Appalachians like a scream. Orion frowned, for his missile had not struck the heart, and his eye drifted on in search of other prey. The wounded shoulder lay open to the sky, a vast gaping hollow, and the mountain limped onward, carried forward through oceans of time in its long, patient journey to the shore.

THOUGH ADAMS WAS SUSPICIOUS FROM THE BEGINning, it was not immediately apparent to Colonel

Bead that something was wrong. The six-day journey to the Cumberland garrison had tired him considerably and his mind was bent toward arrival, welcome, and the enjoyment of a warm bed. When the road began to narrow, Adams worried they had taken a wrong turn, but Colonel Bead trod on. When they came to the remains of a weeks-dead confederate soldier lying scavenged on the roadside, Adams assumed Union encroachment, but Colonel Bead judged it no more than misfortune. When they came to the crest of a ridge and looked down into a broad, circular bowl of land that stretched between them and the Cumberland Mountain garrison on the other side, Adams had an uneasy feeling about the crater-like valley and suggested they go around it. But Colonel Bead paid him no mind and through the valley they went.

As they descended into the hollow, the road became so narrow that it vanished altogether among weeds and fallen logs and stones strewn across the ground. They found it again only by faithfully maintaining their heading until the path emerged once more from the brush. At length, the land began to slope upward and Colonel Bead's spirits rose with it, for he knew that at the crest of the valley his new garrison awaited, and within it lay the promise of peace and quiet. Adam's followed closely behind, but he suspected an unseen foil to his colonel's hopes.

To Colonel Bead's great perturbation, Adam's was right.

Pop-smack-sizzle. A flurry of splinters erupted from a hickory tree three feet to Colonel Bead's right side. While Adams threw himself to the ground and covered his head with his hands, Colonel Bead turned and inspected the tree curiously as if it had exploded at him in some sort of arboreal insult. He ran his fingers across the grey bark and then used the tip of his index finger to gently test the sharpness of a splinter jutting out of the tree's shattered sapwood.

"Suh, hide you-uh-self!"

Colonel Bead dug into the tree's soft, exposed flesh with his fingernail and pried out an impacted musket ball.

"Would you look at that, Adams? They've shot at us."

"I puh-ray they don't shoot again, suh. I beg you get down."

Colonel Bead turned away from the tree and looked up the hill toward the garrison. "They've mistaken us for Union scouts, I expect. Come on, Adams."

Adam's stayed put while Colonel Bead went on. After he had taken three steps—*pop-smack-sizzle*—another innocent hickory exploded. Adams said, "Damn!" and pulled his pistol out and looked around for something to shoot.

"Lay down your arms and surrender!" A young blue-capped Union soldier raised his head above a redoubt some thirty yards further up the hill and pointed his musket at Adams. Adams dropped his pistol into the dirt and raised his hands in the air to show he meant it. Colonel Bead observed all this with growing confusion.

"Get on the ground," cried the Union soldier. "I'll shoot you."

"How did he get up there, Adams?" said Colonel Bead. He slumped to his knees and looked from Adams to the soldier ponderously.

"Quiet!" The young soldier stood from behind the redoubt and walked toward them with his musket

shouldered. He narrowed one eye and sighted down the gun-barrel, laying a sure aim on Colonel Bead. "I got me a colonel!" he yelled. The heads of three more soldiers sprouted from the redoubt and peered down the hill like curious rabbits. "I seen him first. I seen 'em both."

"Can I have one of them," said one of the sprouts.

"You think they got any more," said another.

"They-uh ah but two of us," said Adams.

"What did he say?"

"He said they wasn't but two."

"I seen 'em first," said the musket-wielding soldier as he kicked Adams' pistol out of reach. "They both of them mine. Get up."

Adams stood up and kept his hands in the air.

"I am a colonel of the Army of Tennessee, and I demand to be taken to the garrison commander. There's no need to bring the war out here. Let's all sit down at the mess tent and have a cup of coffee. How does that sound?"

The sprouts looked at one another in silence, then at the soldier in the road, then back at the colonel. "That old man crazy," one of them said.

"A mighty fine idea, colonel. Let's go on up to the garrison and have some coffee. You lead on." The solider with the musket stepped behind the colonel and Adams and waited.

As Colonel Bead marched toward the garrison, he smiled and said over his shoulder, "That wasn't so bad was it, Adams?"

Adams sighed and shook his head. "No, suh."

When he passed under the Union flag raised over the gate of the Cumberland Mountain garrison, Colonel Bead's confusion began to clear. When he was marched past the mess tent without any offer of hospitality, he began to doubt that coffee was forthcoming. When his subsequent questions and demands went unanswered and laughed-at, he began to feel indignant. But when he was pushed unceremoniously into a fenced kennel furnished only with a lean-to, a fire pit, and an uncouth bucket, he finally began to understand that he had become a prisoner of war. In fact, the Union had dislodged the Army of Tennessee from the garrison only a few weeks before, news of which would either trouble or amuse General Felix Zollicoffer when he found out—Colonel Bead wasn't sure which. He took some comfort, however, in the fact that he had maintained the company of Lieutenant Adams in this new trial—though this provided little comfort to Adams himself, who preferred to have been shot.

Within their kennel, they discovered three other men huddled beneath the lean-to. There seemed nothing human about them save their eyes, which stood out from their emaciated faces like fat grubs in rotten wood. Faint clouds of vapor puffed from each of six withered nostrils. The grey tatters of their Confederate uniforms hung from their limbs like grave-wrappings.

Colonel Bead knelt in front of the three wasted men and looked into their unseeing eyes. He touched one of the six knobby knees and shook it gently, but it only clattered against the other like a dried branch swayed by the wind. "Hello, I say. Are you boys here long?" No glimmer of recognition or conscious thought stirred their silence and the six eyes maintained their sightless stare.

"What's happened to them, suh?"

The colonel frowned and tenderly touched one of the wasted cheeks. A corps badge dangled from the shoulder of the boy's uniform and Colonel Bead tugged it free and rubbed it between his fingers thoughtfully. "They are poor boys who should have gone to the sea, Adams. They should have followed a star."

Twice each day, a guard threw a handful of hardtack over the fence and dropped a bucket of watery broth at the gate so they could sop the hardtack in it and eat. Adams saw that the three "scarecrows," as he called them, did not move even for food. Colonel Bead tried to feed them by force but withdrew in defeat. The scarecrows never stirred and never ceased in their wide-eyed watch, and after the third week of their captivity, neither Colonel Bead nor

Adams could account for the life that maintained them; they neither ate nor drank and yet the vapor of their breath in the cold air never changed: it neither quickened nor slowed, but only went on steadily and without purpose like the silent gaze of their protuberant eyes.

"It's unnatural, suh."

"Is it?" asked Colonel Bead.

"No man can live without food or what-uh."

"Who's to say what's natural, Adams? I can never tell. My father once told me that there are corners of the ocean where fish leap out of the water, flapping their fins like wings, and they soar into the sky and sing like birds. I told him that it sounded strange but he said it was the most natural thing in the world. What do you think, Adams?"

"I don't know, suh."

"I don't either. But I'd like to. Sometimes I think there's too much to know and more to see than any man can ever manage, and it doesn't seem fair somehow. Maybe that's why the scarecrows stare, Adams. Maybe they've got it right. Maybe they see everything, everything there is—and they can't bear even to blink for they'll miss the best part and break the spell and never get to the end of it all. Maybe that's it, Adams. Move out of the way. Let them see."

Adams moved aside and Colonel Bead sat down beside the scarecrows and drew up his knees like one of them and looked where they looked. He stared for a long time but saw only the kennel's fence before him and the Union guards beyond and the grey mountain looming in the distance. He joined in the endless watch until his eyelids grew heavy and he slept.

When morning came, Adams stood at the kennel gate and shouted. He demanded more and better food. He demanded clean water. He jumped up and down and cried for warmer blankets. He cursed every Union soldier he saw and spat at them until they moved out of spittle range. He screamed for paper and pen and the chance to write to his wife and children. He spewed and roared and growled until Colonel Bead entreated him to come away and be calm.

"It's beastly, Adams. Be a gentleman. The war won't last. We've only to abide it while it does."

Adams tried to say "Yes, suh," but he'd undone his voice and only made a gurgling sound.

"Did I ever tell you that my father was a prisoner, Adams? He said he fell afoul of pirates once and they sold him off to the owner of an Antarctic diamond mine. He took great pride in the fact that he was sold for twice the sum of his fellow prisoners owing to his strong arms, his resilience in extreme cold, and his ability to see in the dark like a cat—which made him perfect for Antarctic mining. He said that for two years he never saw the sun except as it shone in the diamonds he found, for an Antarctic diamond catches starlight no matter where it is and shines out even in complete darkness. Did you know that, Adams?

Adam's gurgled and raised a doubtful eyebrow.

"He was stuck in that mine so long he forgot what warmth felt like. His right hand froze solid and he used it for a rock hammer to beat gems out of the earth, and the jewels he hewed out were wonders of the world. He uncovered a diamond the size of a human head. It lit up the whole mine like the sun had risen in the deeps of it." Adams nodded his head dutifully. "He couldn't keep what he found, of course, which was terrible unfortunate for my mother.

"But in time his captain did free him. She refitted the *Esprit de la Mer* for icebreaking, which was why she had to leave him so long in the mine. He said the ship arrived like a battering ram smashing the ice and shattering it like china glass. His red-haired captain played a fiddle tune that put the guards to sleep and she stole away with my father and all his fellows." Colonel Bead paused and sighed and looked

up at the mountain. "Wouldn't that be something, Adams? To be stolen away?"

Adams nodded and smiled at the colonel as one does a grandparent who no longer understands the present and instead retreats into the familiar company of the past. That night the colonel sat again beside the scarecrows and joined them in their watch until he slept.

The autumn air crisped and nipped, and every day it licked harder at the colonel's ears and nose. His captors paid him no more mind than a stray dog, and as the temperature plumbed lower and lower depths, Adams cried out for firewood and coffee and blankets and hot bacon and daily newspapers and cards. Adams yelled for three straight days until a Union sergeant threw him a charred log and made him beg for an ember with which to kindle it. Adams tenderly blew on the ember and coaxed it to life and he and Colonel Bead gathered around the single ruby–hued gem of warmth and thawed themselves as thankfully as if they were gathered at the burning bush of Moses. Thereafter, a guard delivered a single log and a glowing ember each day and

Adams treated them each as if they were treasures of unspeakable price.

Each morning, the colonel inspected the scarecrows. He snapped his fingers at them and waved his hand in front of their faces. He whispered into their ears and slipped his hand into their shirts to feel the beating of their hearts. They abided his molestations without protest or reflex and maintained their unblinking stare into space. Each day, the colonel sat with them longer and longer. He assumed their posture, drawing up his knees and slumping his head forward like a buzzard and peeling his eyes wide to stare into the distance and see what they saw.

"Come and watch with us, Adams," said Colonel Bead as he sidled up next to the outermost scarecrow. "The yelling and carrying on will do no good. Come and watch."

Adams' lip turned up in abhorrence. "No, suh. It isn't natural." As he looked at the colonel he saw that he could no longer easily tell his commanding officer apart from the other scarecrows. His face had thinned in captivity and his uniform was worn thin; soon it would be in tatters. When the colonel assumed the position of his watch, he seemed only a degree or two more lively than the withering creatures beside him. But Adams said nothing more and did not protest the colonel's watch. Instead he removed the buckle of his belt and began to scrape at the base of the gatepost.

Colonel Bead awoke in the night. An eerie howl of wind startled him and he jerked upright. At his side, the scarecrows watched, their breaths puffing in quiet white billows. Adams leaned against the gatepost, snoring. The colonel crossed his arms and rubbed his shoulders. He chattered his terrible teeth and blinked the sleep from his eyes. He leaned his head back and wondered how close was morning, and then he looked up into the Gap and saw a mist pour through it and gather up into a cloud that flowed and swirled like a gossamer gown. Beneath the hem of the gown a white sheet of rain descended and froze the earth wherever it fell. In the moonlight the sheeting rain looked to Colonel Bead like an ivory foot moving surely and uncaringly beneath a cloudy raiment. The heel pressed into the trees of the Cumberland Gap and rocked forward as the toes settled onto the vales and fingers of the mountain pass and iced them in white crystal. A freezing gale blew across the garrison and Colonel Bead shivered and watched with the scarecrows and dared not blink, and he saw what few men ever have: the coming of the White Lady. She stepped down out of the sky, descending slowly, her movements imperceptible to anyone not trained to look long and hard into the smooth, calculated precision of her advance. But Colonel Bead had learned to see and he watched with unblinking eyes. She lit upon the earth as a young girl slips out of her bed and onto the cold floor. She covered the treetops and Appalachian balds in her cottony robe and draped her lace across the valley. As the colonel watched, she raised a gelid finger to her lips and—*ssshhhhhhhh*—her frigid whisper cascaded across the land and swept away the lingering scents and sights of autumn.

When Adams woke the next morning, the ground was covered in snow. He cried for an ember and kindled the fire and turned to wake his colonel but found him un-asleep. Colonel Bead had taken up the stare of the scarecrows in earnest. His jaw hung slack and his eyes were engaged on the mountain.

"Look at me, suh!"

Adams shook Colonel Bead and the colonel's irises pin-wheeled into points. He blinked. "Good morning, Adams." Adams sighed in relief.

"Come to the fi-uh, suh." Adam held out his hand to assist Colonel Bead to his feet, but the colonel turned away. He crawled in front of the scarecrows and stared at them.

"The poor boy," said Colonel Bead. One of the scarecrows had frozen solid. His skin had turned a purple-grey color and his eyes, having seen their last, were closed. Colonel Bead pulled at the boy's arm. "Help me move him by the fire, Adams. We can thaw him."

"No, suh," Adams said.

"Adams, we must. The boy needs help, can't you see?"

Adams pulled the colonel away. "Let him be, suh. I'll see to him." While Colonel Bead rubbed his hands over the meager fire and hummed, Adams dragged the dead man away from his brethren. The boy was frozen stiff, right through to the middle, and Adams had to maneuver the cadaver by degrees. He flipped him end to end, and rolled him, and flopped him, until he upended the poor boy out of sight behind the lean-to.

Four days later, Lieutenant Adams and Colonel Bead observed signs of festivity in the heart of the garrison. Though no one informed them directly, the two men deduced from the smell of roasting hams and steaming ciders and the distant sounds of merriment that Christmas had come to the Cumberland Gap. In the late afternoon a Union captain with formidable mustaches presented himself at the gate with a bundle of firewood and a freshly skinned rabbit. He didn't speak, but whether by the illusion of his sharply curled mustaches or by genuine goodwill, he seemed to smile as he delivered his gifts.

"Thank you, captain," said Colonel Bead. The captain haltingly saluted the colonel and departed without breaking his silence.

Adams prepared the feast and the two men ate. Adams tried to engage Colonel Bead in a Christmas carol, but the colonel turned aside his attempts and stared nervously at the mountain pass as evening fell.

"Would you some mo-uh rabbit, suh?" Adams tore off a haunch and held it out in expectation. Colonel Bead waved it off, parrying the leg of beast as surely as an enemy's blow. Adams spat into the fire. He put the rabbit leg into his mouth, clapped his lips over it, and pulled the bone out clean.

As Adams squatted beside the fire and chewed his game, Colonel Bead pulled his coat close around him. He took his seat beside the scarecrows and looked out beyond the firelight into the darkness. Adams turned away and reached for the last of the rabbit, and when he turned back, three scarecrows stared at him, not two. The colonel had blended into their number completely.

"Colonel Bead, suh?"

The colonel did not answer.

"Colonel Bead, suh?" Adams frowned and rubbed his neck and chewed his rabbit ponderously. Then he slipped out his belt buckle and sat down beside the gatepost. While Union soldiers filled the tents and shanty buildings with merry notes of Christmas, the only sound outside in the biting cold was the *scrape, scrape, scrape* of brass against wood.

When the sun came up, there was a new fall of snow on the ground and the second scarecrow had turned into an ice block. He was frozen through like the first and had a thick spike of ice hanging down from his nose. The spike had grown so long that it had frozen to the ground between the scarecrow's legs. He looked very like a crystal statue of an elephantine Hindu diety that Adams had once seen in a sideshow in Atlanta. Adams stared at the spectacle in bewilderment and chose not to bother chipping him free of the ground to roll him out of sight. Instead, Adams knelt in front of Colonel Bead. The old man stared through him.

"Colonel?" Adams took the colonel by the shoulders and shook him but his stare didn't waver. Adams shook him harder and still the old man stared. Adams took his belt buckle in one hand and Colonel Bead's arm in the other. He put the ragged metal edge of the buckle against the cold white skin of the forearm. "I am sorry, suh." He drew the metal across the colonel's skin, opening a cut an inch long. A viscous bead of blood seeped out of the wound.

"Adams?"

"Yes, suh."

"My arm hurts, Adams."

"Yes, suh. It's but a scratch, suh."

"What's that, Adams?"

"Come to the fi-uh, suh."

"The fire?"

"Yes, suh."

The colonel broke free of the scarecrows' watch and crawled to the fire. Adams sat beside him and leaned his body against his colonel's and rubbed his arms and legs. "Tell me a story about you-uh fath-uh, suh. Tell me about the sea."

"The sea?"

"Yes, suh."

"The sea. The sea. I scarcely remember it, Adams. You must go to see it someday."

"Yes, suh. I will, suh. Warm you-uh hands at the fi-uh, colonel. It's warm, see?" Adams pulled Colonel Bead's hands from his lap and pushed them toward the flame. "Like so, colonel." He showed the colonel how to rub his hands together and hold them close enough to the fire to thaw. The colonel's glassy eyes wheeled into focus and his mind warmed as his hands did. He became himself again.

"Thank you, Adams." The old man's face flushed with a tinge of shame.

"Yes, suh." When he was satisfied that the colonel was in possession of his wits, Adams moved to the gatepost. *Scrape-scrape-scrape.*

Colonel Bead huddled by the fire and clapped his hands for warmth and muttered to himself. "She's seen me. She's coming. She's coming over the mountain. Never should have left the sea." He nodded to himself and continued his muttering and often turned to look at the single remaining scarecrow. "Do you see her?" he'd ask. He'd wait for an answer but when none came he'd turn back to the fire and clap his hands and moan and fall into indistinct murmurs that Adams could not make out. *Scrape-scrape-scrape.*

There was no firewood that day, and no broth, nor any bread, and no soldier stirred in the garrison. Adams laid the leftover bones of the previous day's rabbit in the embers of the fire until they were brittle. He ate what he could and ground the rest to meal in his mouth. He fed the meal to Colonel Bead who could not have managed the bones with his awful teeth. Neither man spoke to the other and they watched the last gleam of the ruby embers fade away in chilling silence.

"She'll come, Adams."

"Who will, suh?"

"Watch for her. Come sit with me." Colonel Bead crawled to the scarecrow's side and assumed the position of the watch.

"No, suh. Come away from they-uh."

"I saw her, Adams. I saw her."

"Colonel, we ah leaving." Adams walked to the gate. He looked through the fence and listened. There was no movement in the garrison, and no sound. With one swift kick of his boot, the base of the gatepost snapped where he had nearly sawn through it with his buckle. "Come, colonel. Let's go."

"What?"

Adams pulled Colonel Bead up by the arm and dragged him toward the gate.

"It's no use, Adams. What are you doing?"

Adams pulled the gatepost upward, creating a gap of about a foot under the bottom wire of the fence. "Und-uh, colonel."

Colonel Bead sputtered in confusion, but he obeyed. He wriggled under the wire and once on the other side he stood up and looked in bafflement at Adams as he scuffled under the fence like a panicked animal. Adams leaped to his feet and crouched over, ready to run. His eyes darted across the garrison, inspecting each shadow and corner for any eyes that might have spotted them. He grabbed Colonel Bead by the arm and rushed through the unbroken snow to the corner of the nearest tent. As Adams looked around the edge of the tent toward the garrison's gate, Colonel Bead looked behind them. They'd disturbed a wide trench of snow and it led the colonel's eyes back to the kennel gate; just beyond it he could see the scarecrow staring at him.

"The poor boy should have followed a star."

Adams jerked the colonel's arm and they ran toward the garrison's main entry. Icy wind howled in the treetops and a fresh snow began to fall. Adams pulled up short and leaned against a dead tree. He looked around madly for signs of pursuit, but nothing moved in the camp. There was no campfire lit, no light in any tent, no hint of distant conversation or laughter. Only the mournful keening of the wind filled the empty space of the garrison.

"Good god," said Colonel Bead. Adams turned toward the colonel sharply, his eyes alert. The colonel put out his hand and stroked the dead tree beside Adams' face. "The poor boy," he muttered. Adams stepped back in horror. A Union soldier stood upright beside him, caught firmly in the position of attention where the winter had frozen him to the ground. Adams backed away and looked around the courtyard. It wasn't empty. He had failed to see it clearly. It was a crowd of activity that had been stopped, seized, and held captive by the sudden advent of winter. Men stood at their posts, hard as brick, covered in snow and long, sharp sickles of ice. Some were frozen with their rifles shouldered, the barrels

jutting up like dead branches in the wind. Others had been arrested in moments of laughter, heads thrown back, mouths open, teeth glimmering under layers of ice. One man sat atop his warhorse; he had drawn his sword and pointed it up at the mountain pass as if he had seen his enemy and ordered a last desperate charge—but before his moment of glory, he'd been caught and enshrined like a memorial.

Adams stumbled backward, eyes wide. The courtyard had become a statuary of horrors. He grabbed Colonel Bead and dragged him through the garrison gate. The wind whistled across the Stars and Stripes and they also were held captive, frozen mid-flap in the grip of the White Lady.

The colonel stumbled behind Adams as they ran. A deep blanket of snow covered the road and they had to stop every fifty yards to examine the sur-rounding trees and gauge the lay of the road between them. The wind screamed.

"Do you hear it?" Colonel Bead shouted.

Adams ignored him. He dragged his colonel blindly into the crater-like valley before the garrison. When he stopped, he looked up the slope behind them, still suspicious of pursuit, then turned back and spotted the place they'd been captured. The snow was heaped up against the redoubt and three soldiers stared at them. They were frozen in the act of rising as if, having heard the approach of some unimaginable calamity, they had stood to meet it and had been entombed in the instant of its revelation. Adams ran, stubbornly hauling Colonel Bead in tow. When they reached the trough of the valley, Colonel Bead stumbled and fell.

"Get up, suh. Get up!"

"Where's the road, Adams? Do you see it?"

Barren trees studded the land around them. The ice-sheathed trunks stabbed into the air, dark and withered and evenly spaced, giving them no sign at all of a well-traveled road. The line of their trail through the snow curled down from the northern rise and ended abruptly at Colonel Bead's feet like a question mark.

"Do you hear that, Adams?

Adams ran forward. He kicked at the snowbank. He dug and burrowed and struck the weed-covered ground and cursed. He ran to the right and cleared the snow again. "Find the road, colonel!" He spun and ran and burrowed again finding only rock and frozen brush beneath the snow.

Colonel Bead watched Adams commotion in wonder and began to laugh. "We've got off it, Adams.

We've got off it at last!" Then the colonel too began to kick at the snow and shovel it with his hands. He smiled like a boy tearing into a long-awaited gift. He flung snow right and left. He beat at it and tore at it and hurled it away from him and laughed. Then he stopped abruptly and stared at the ground. He bent over and picked up a small conical stone and turned it in his fingers.

"She's coming, Adams." The colonel tossed the strange stone to Adams and looked up at the horizon.

"I told you I could hear it."

The wind squalled around them, pulling the snow from the sky and lashing their skin, raking them with a million tiny blades. Adams inspected the stone. It fit easily into the palm of his hand and was shaped by hundreds of v-shaped radiations originating at one end and spreading out along its length. It looked like rays of light fossilized and held captive in cold stone. "What is it, suh?" yelled Adams. The icy gale tore his words from his mouth and hurled them into the distance.

"It's a shatter-cone."

"A what, suh?"

"It means we've followed the right road, Adams. And we've arrived. Don't you hear it?" Colonel Bead smiled and tilted his ear to the eastern horizon.

"Damn it, suh! We will die out he-uh!" Adams hurled the stone into the wind and the wind whispered back—*sssshhhhhhhh!* He saw a tower rise up in the Gap of the mountain, a misty column of vapor that swirled and danced like a woman robed in silk. Then for a moment the wind stuttered. It slackened and swirled as if it had met with some immovable force through which it could not pass and could only go around. In that instant, Adams heard something that sounded like a note. He looked at Colonel Bead, who raised an eyebrow and grinned. The wind eddied again, creating a momentary stillness in which Colonel Bead and Lieutenant Adams were free of cold and wind and noise and were shrouded instead by the bright, warmth of music.

When the eddy passed, Colonel Bead's face broke into a shape that he could not remember ever having formed before. It was a smile of purest delight, a smile that breaks only upon those who have looked long and, having looked, have learned at last to see.

From the east, the Appalachian Mountains heaved up against the clouds. The winter wind drove against them, covering them in white water and sending it spraying over the caps of the high peaks in great plumes. Then, amid the violence of the storm, a tall white form rose above the saddle between two crags. It was a sail. Its mast tilted and swayed and climbed upward until Colonel Bead and Lieutenant Adams could see a fair ship at the crest of the ridge. It tottered on the ledge as its sails luffed. Its lines screamed in the gale. Then it seemed that something in the nature of the ship pushed back against the wind. The sails punched full. Colonel Bead and Lieutenant Adams heard again a sharp, playful measure of music sweep past and the ship began to tilt. With an illusory sluggishness the ship rocked forward onto the face of the mountain and descended along its curve. It rushed earthward like the calving of a glacier and vanished momentarily into the valley before exploding up the slope of the opposite ridge and leaping into the air, barely able to contain the power that drove it. Music was everywhere. It filled the sails of the ship's main, mizzen, and foremasts, each set with its full complement of cloth, as the vessel thundered across the mountain steeps.

"I told you she would come, Adams."

Adams had no reply. He stared dumbfounded while the ship altered its tack and turned toward them.

"Are you ready to go?" asked Colonel Bead.

"Whey-uh ah we going, suh?"

Colonel Bead smiled as the ship slipped gracefully down into the crater-valley. The sounds of fiddle music filled the air and though he could see the fury of the White Lady raging in the Gap, the crater was calm and warm and peaceful. The ship slowed and a man stepped to the rail. He cast a rope down which landed at Adams feet.

"After you, lieutenant," said Colonel Bead.

Adams, still slack-jawed, took hold of the rope and the crew hauled him aboard. When the rope was thrown back out for Colonel Bead, he took hold of it fiercely and looked up. The man at the rail smiled as he hauled Barnabas aboard. From behind his smile, a single bright tooth twinkled and shone.

"Hold fast!" cried the bright-toothed man.

The air around the ship exploded with music. Colonel Bead turned and saw a woman at the helm; her hair shimmered and rippled like flames. She held a golden fiddle in the cleft of her neck. Beside her a tall man with a thin beard and a kind face smiled at her as he watched her play. He looked up at the sails, then across the starboard rail at the raging storm issuing through the Gap.

"Play well, cherie," he said in an accent that sounded to Colonel Bead like a frenchman's, then he turned away and shouted to the crew. "Get underway. Prepare to tack. Lay a course three degrees east of the Pleiades. Rough sea ahead, gentlemen. Ready yourselves."

The great ship heaved over. Music filled the sails and drove them. Colonel Bead stepped to the rail and looked down. Below him he spotted the well-trodden road. The ship turned away from it and gathered speed and fled the valley as the White Lady howled in their wake. Barnabas Alan Bead did not look down again.

ALSO FROM RABBIT ROOM PRESS

THE FIDDLER'S GUN
by A. S. Peterson

FIDDLER'S GREEN
by A. S. Peterson

THE WILDERKING TRILOGY
by Jonathan Rogers

THE WINGFEATHER SAGA
by Andrew Peterson

THE LAST SWEET MILE
by Allen Levi

These and more available at
www.RabbitRoom.com
and wherever great books are sold.

RABBIT ROOM
— PRESS —
NASHVILLE, TENNESSEE